Play Ball!

Adaptation by Marcy Goldberg Sacks

Based on a TV series teleplay written by Susan Kim

Based on the characters created by Susan Meddaugh

HOUGHTON MIFFLIN HARCOURT
Boston • New York • 2009

For information about permission to reproduce selections from this book, write to Permissions, Houghton Mifflin Harcourt Publishing Company, 215 Park Avenue South, New York, New York 10003.

Green Light Readers and its logo are trademarks of Houghton Mifflin Harcourt Publishing Company.

Library of Congress Cataloging-in-Publication Data is on file.

ISBN: 978-0-547-21061-2

Design by Stephanie Cooper and Bill Smith Studio

www.hmhbooks.com
www.marthathetalkingdog.com

Manufactured in China
LEO 10 9 8 7 6 5 4 3 2 1

Martha loves to play catch.

She asks her friend Truman to throw the ball to her.

"Sorry, Martha," says Truman. "I don't want to play."

"I want to be a hobo," Truman says.
"My book says hobos ride on trains.
They even sleep outdoors.
Would you like to come with me?"

"Sounds like fun!" says Martha.
"When can we go?
I have to be home for dinner."

But Truman tells her,
"Hobos never come home."
Martha is worried.
"Why do you want to
leave home?"

"We have a softball game
tomorrow," says Truman.
"The coach says I have to play.
But I can't catch the ball!"
"Barking bloopers!" says Martha.
"I'll give you catching lessons.

All it takes is practice.
Trust me—I'm an expert!"

Martha and Truman go to the park.
They see their friends.
They see Alice throw a ball to Skits.

"Skits is an expert ball catcher too,"
says Martha.
"And Alice is an expert thrower."

Alice throws the ball to Truman.
"Don't be afraid of the ball!"
she says.

"The ball is your friend," Martha
tells him.
"Right, Skits?"
Skits says, "Woof!"

Alice throws the ball again.
"Try to keep your eye on the ball,"
Martha says.

Whoosh. Plop. Drop.
The ball hits Truman's glove and falls out.
"Squeeze the glove," Martha says.

They practice all day.
Toss. Miss. Toss. Miss. Toss.
Catch!

Finally Truman holds on to
the ball.
Alice and Helen cheer.
Martha is a good coach.

The next day Truman stands
in the outfield.
Smack! The ball is in the air.
It is headed right to him.

Truman keeps his eye on the ball.
He puts up his glove.
"The ball is my friend," he says.

Plop. Squeeze. Hooray!
Truman catches the ball.

"Throw the ball to second base,"
someone yells.
Oh no.
Truman is not an expert thrower.

"Martha, can you teach me how to
throw the ball?" Truman asks.
"Sorry," Martha says. "Dogs can't
throw. No thumbs."

Match the picture to the word.

Glove

Throw

Catch

Coach

Help Truman learn to catch by filling in the blanks. Choose from the following words:

LESSONS   EFFORT   CATCH   FRIENDS
GLOVE   BALL   THROW   COACH   HIT

Truman did not know how to _____.

Martha gave Truman catching _____.

Martha told Truman to be _____ with the ball.

Truman made an _____ to practice.

It is important to keep your eye on the _____.

The batter _____ the ball in the air.

Truman raised his _____ to catch it.

Martha is a good catching _____.

But Martha does not know how to _____ the ball.